Tons Of Tools
To Help Me Be Me!

By Author & Illustrator: Farrah Raines

DEDICATED TO ALL THE AMAZING PEOPLE IN MY LIFE
MY HUSBAND TODD, MY GUARDIAN ANGEL DAD,
& MY DEAR FRIENDS

Thank you to all the people who believed in me from the past and the present.
Who encourage me to follow my dreams, and to never doubt my abilities!

Ollie the owl says, "Whooooo wants to play?" Nelly the ostrich is to nervous, and Seymour the snail is to tired to play.

Ollie the owl thought to himself, "My friends need to learn tools to help them feel better. I know who can help them!"

Tyson Turtle can help my friend Nelly learn calming tools. Robo Rabbit is really good at teaching alerting tools that can help my friend Seymour stay awake.

Nelly wandered up to the pond to find Tyson turtle floating around.
"Oh dear oh dear I am so nervous I just feel like hiding my head", said Nelly!
"Not to worry I can teach you some tools to help you calm down", said Tyson turtle.

Slow your mind and body down by doing

your favorite yoga poses.

Listen to music that makes you feel calm.

Having someone roll a big exercise ball up and down your back can be very relaxing.

Counting slowly can be a great tool to help you calm down.

Deep breathing is another great calm down tool to use when you feel nervous. Using pinwheels or feathers is a fun way to practice breathing.

Seymour the snail was tired of feeling sleepy all
the time. "Robo rabbit will you teach me how to
feel more awake?", said Seymour. " I have just the
tools for you!", said Robo.

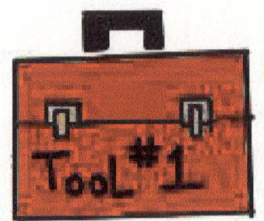

We can wake our bodies up by bouncing

on an exercise ball.

Eating crunchy snacks like carrots

or celery sticks will wake your

mouth up.

Hopping like a rabbit or using a trampoline

to jump will help your body wake up.

Go outside and get your body moving. Take a walk, play tag. or roll a ball to a friend.

Turn some music on and have a dance party!

Feeling better Nelly and Seymour wanted to play with their friend Ollie the owl. Before they started to play both friends could not wait to share the tools that they had learned. Ollie knew that this would be a good way for his friends to practice their tools. So the three friends spent the rest of the day having fun trying all the calming and alerting tools.

We have our toolboxes full with tools. Now it is your turn.
What tools help you feel better?

THE END

Calming Tools

Tool #1: Do your favorite yoga pose.

Tool #2: Listen to music that makes you feel calm.

Tool #3: Have someone roll a exercise ball up and down your back.

Tool #4: Slowly count 1 to 10.

Tool #5: Practice deep breathing strategies such as pinwheel or feather breathing.

<u>Alerting Tools</u>

Tool #1: Bounce on an exercise ball.

Tool #2: Eat a crunchy snack like carrots or celery sticks.

Tool #3: Hopping like a rabbit or jumping on a trampoline.

Tool#4: Go outside and get your body moving.

Tool#5: Turn some music on and have a dance party.

ABOUT THE AUTHOR

Author Farrah Raines is an pediatric occupational therapy assistant, license massage therapist, children's yoga & mindfulness instructor, color guard instructor, author, illustrator, and public speaker. She has an extensive background in the treatment of children and adolescents with autism and sensory processing disorders. Check out her YouTube Channel Miss Farrah's Movement and Fun for more therapy related activities for children.

www.ingramcontent.com/pod-product-compliance
Lightning Source LLC
Chambersburg PA
CBHW041010170626
46815CB00002B/248